CW01460677

EX LIBRIS

VINTAGE CLASSICS

GUNNAR GUNNARSSON

ADVENT

TRANSLATED FROM THE DANISH BY
Philip Roughton

WITH AN AFTERWORD BY
Jón Kalman Stefánsson

VINTAGE CLASSICS

1 3 5 7 9 10 8 6 4 2

Vintage Classics is part of the Penguin Random House group of companies

Vintage, Penguin Random House UK, One Embassy Gardens, 8 Viaduct Gardens, London sw11 7bw

penguin.co.uk/vintage-classics
global.penguinrandomhouse.com

Penguin
Random House
UK

This edition published in Vintage Classics in 2025
First published in Denmark by Gyldendalske Boghandel Nordisk Forlag in 1936

Copyright © Gunnar Gunnarsson 1936
Translation copyright © Philip Roughton 2025
Afterword copyright © Jón Kalman Stefánsson 2006
Afterword translation copyright © Philip Roughton 2025

The moral right of the copyright holders has been asserted

Penguin Random House values and supports copyright. Copyright fuels creativity, encourages diverse voices, promotes freedom of expression and supports a vibrant culture. Thank you for purchasing an authorised edition of this book and for respecting intellectual property laws by not reproducing, scanning or distributing any part of it by any means without permission. You are supporting authors and enabling Penguin Random House to continue to publish books for everyone. No part of this book may be used or reproduced in any manner for the purpose of training artificial intelligence technologies or systems. In accordance with Article 4(3) of the DSM Directive 2019/790, Penguin Random House expressly reserves this work from the text and data mining exception.

Typeset in 14.2/17pt Bembo Book MT Pro by Six Red Marbles UK, Thetford, Norfolk
Printed and bound in Great Britain by Clays Ltd, Elcograf S.p.A.

The authorised representative in the EEA is Penguin Random House Ireland,
Morrison Chambers, 32 Nassau Street, Dublin D02 YH68

A CIP catalogue record for this book is available from the British Library

ISBN 9781529963076

Penguin Random House is committed to a sustainable future
for our business, our readers and our planet. This book is made
from Forest Stewardship Council® certified paper.

MIX
Paper | Supporting
responsible forestry
FSC
www.fsc.org
FSC® C018179

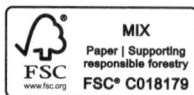

As a feast day draws near, everyone prepares for it in their own way. Many different approaches are taken, and Benedikt had his own too. It consisted of his leaving home at the start of Yule, preferably on Advent Sunday itself, weather permitting, amply equipped with provisions – a few changes of socks and several pairs of newly stitched leather shoes in his rucksack, along with a Primus stove, a can of paraffin and a small bottle of methylated spirits – and heading into the mountains, where at this time of the year only winter's hardy raptors, foxes and a few stray sheep roamed. It was precisely those wandering sheep that he was after, sheep that had been overlooked during the three regular roundups of the autumn. They certainly couldn't be allowed to freeze or starve to death in those high places simply because no one bothered or dared to seek them out and bring them home. They too were living creatures. And he bore a certain responsibility for them. His goal was quite simple: to find them and bring them home safe and sound before the great feast day sanctified the earth and brought peace and contentment to the hearts of those who have done all that they are able to do.

On this Advent expedition of his, Benedikt was always alone. Truly alone? He had no human companions, in any case. He was, however, accompanied by his dog, and most often, his leader sheep. His dog at the time of this story was named Leó – a veritable pope, Benedikt called him. Due to his toughness, the leader sheep, a wether, was called Eitill.[*]

For a number of years, these three had been inseparable when it came to such treks and had gradually got to know each other, inside and out, with the in-depth familiarity that is perhaps only obtainable between completely unrelated species of animals, such that no shadow of one's own self, one's own blood, own wishes or desires confuses or obscures things. There was, incidentally, usually a fourth member of the group, the good horse Faxi, who unfortunately was

[*] The Icelandic word *eitill* means 'knot' (as in a knot in wood) or 'node'. Something that is *eitilharður* is extremely hard in texture.

too slender-legged and heavy-bodied to trudge through early winter's deep drifts of soft snow, and what's more, was hardly fit to withstand so many strenuous days on the meagre rations with which the others made do. It was with sadness and regret that Benedikt and Leó parted from him, even if it was only for a week. Eitill took this twist like everything else: more stoically.

There that threesome went now, this winter day: in front was Leó, with the tip of his tongue sticking contentedly out of the right corner of his mouth despite the cold. Behind him was Eitill, even-tempered as always, and finally Benedikt, lugging his skis. Down here in the farmland, the snow was still too light and loose to carry a skier; he had no choice but to trudge through it, and of course ended up stubbing his toes on tussocks and rocks – oof. It was a fairly heavy slog, but it could have been worse. Leó had lots to look into, as dogs usually do, and was in high spirits. At times he couldn't contain himself and simply had to let it out, bounding away and kicking up a cloud of snow behind him towards Benedikt, barking at him, jumping up at him and clamouring for praise and petting.

Yes, you're a veritable pope, Benedikt would remark. That was his term of endearment for his comrade; higher praise couldn't come from his mouth.

For the moment, they were making their way through the settlement towards Botn, the farm lying nearest the mountains. They had the whole day ahead of them and took it easy, following the path from farm to farm, stopping and greeting people and dogs, but a cup of coffee, no thank you, not today – we'd like to get there in good time. Instead, they had some milk – all three. Time and again, Benedikt was questioned about his outlook on the weather. People didn't mean to be nosy or come across as doomsayers, they simply asked – as was their right, of course. And someone might add afterwards: Yes, what I wanted to say was, Leó must be the kind of dog who's good at finding the way, even in darkness and snow? It was said almost jokingly, eyes fixed on the ground to avoid alluding to the sky's somewhat-threatening clouds, even if only with a glance. And someone else might interject spiritedly: Find the way? That he can certainly do, the mongrel.

All three of us can, Benedikt replied unconcernedly, before finishing his bowl of milk. Thanks for the drink.

Nothing against you and Eitill, but I would rely mainly on Leó, said the farmer, before popping out of the door and fetching a treat for Leó to munch on.

Benedikt made no comment about Leó being a veritable pope, but let the dog know with a nod that he was free to take his time eating the food offered; he could wait that long. Meanwhile, Eitill got a capful of fragrant hay from the farmer's homefield. Then the three of them set off again.

Benedikt hadn't gone to church that day. No, that he hadn't done; there wasn't time for it. In order to reach Botn at a decent hour and get some rest before the following day's early departure and long march, he'd had to make the best use of the day, starting early that morning. It was mainly out of consideration for Eitill that he set a gentle pace this first day. Not that Eitill couldn't cope with going faster or didn't live up to his name. But Benedikt had to be careful not to overexert the wether from the start. That's why he couldn't very well make a detour to the church. Every Advent Sunday, it was this amble of his through the settlement towards the mountains that was his churchgoing. What's more, before he left home, he'd sat on his bed in the family room and read the day's scripture passage, Matthew 21, concerning Jesus's entry into Jerusalem. But the ringing of the bells, the singing of hymns in the small turf-covered church and the old priest's wise and sedate exposition of the Gospel, he'd had to imagine. And he had no trouble doing so.

Here he was now, walking in snow, white on all sides as far as the eye could see, a greyish-white winter sky, even the ice on the lake was frosted or lightly covered with snow, only the rims of the low craters sticking up here and there drew larger and smaller black rings like a portentous pattern in that snowy waste. But a portent of what? Could it be discovered? Perhaps these crater mouths said: Let everything freeze, stone and water solidify, let the air freeze and sprinkle down as white flakes and lie like a bridal veil, like a shroud over the ground, let the breath freeze in your mouth and the hope in your heart and the blood to death in your veins – deep down, the fire still lives. Perhaps that is what they said. And what, then, did that mean? Perhaps they said something else, too. In any case, apart from those black rings, everything was white, particularly the lake – a glistening white surface, smooth as a dance floor. Who laid it there and invited us to dance?

And as if born of all this whiteness, with the craters' black rings and solitary troll-like lava pillars rising here and there, an air of solemnity marked this Sunday in this settlement near the mountains, something that tugged at the heart. An immeasurable, pure holiness surrounded the placid Sabbath smoke that rose undisturbed from the scattered, low farmhouses that nearly disappeared beneath the snow, an incomprehensible and unimaginably promising stillness. Advent. Advent! Yes . . . Benedikt mouthed the word gingerly, that big, quiet, wonderfully alien yet at the same time homely word, perhaps for Benedikt the most deeply homely of all. Admittedly, he didn't know exactly what it meant, yet there was expectation in it, anticipation, preparation – that much he understood. As the years went by, that one word had come to encompass practically his entire life. For what was his life, what was man's life on earth, if not an imperfect service, sustained by expectation, anticipation, preparation?

They arrived at another farm and the workday

met them with its rural friendliness, but coffee, no thank you, not today, they were in a bit of a hurry, the days were getting shorter, thanks all the same. The farmer considered the sky long and carefully, and frankly didn't think much of the weather prospects. Well, we simply have to take the weather as God gives it, thought Benedikt. The farmer, for his part, could only hope that the storm broke loose before nightfall! Such talk was certainly not to Benedikt's liking, and, well, they had to be going.

Are they of any use, those companions of yours? asked the farmer, reluctant to watch the man go, perhaps seeing him now for the last time, who knows? He'd had such troublesome dreams recently, and these three had a quite-obvious aura of impending ordeals – if not something worse. Isn't Eitill just a millstone round your neck? Can you rely on them, him and the dog?

Can I rely on them? replied Benedikt. All three of us have been through a bit of everything.

A person shouldn't say such things at a perilous hour; mustn't provoke the powers so presumptuously. Making no reply, the farmer let him go, and off they went, the three of them, leaving an uncertain man standing there, chewing tobacco as he watched them walk away, dissatisfied with himself and them and the whole world. Who could understand such people, risking everything – even life itself – for some sheep belonging to someone else? Of the few sheep that Benedikt himself owned, none were missing.

For his part, Benedikt probably had just as little understanding of the prudent farmer. Whatever the case, the three went on. Today was a good day, a good and solemn day, and no one was going to ruin it for him. It was many years ago today that Jesus made his entry into Jerusalem. Knowing this, he could feel, too, how the day had retained a touch of that event over the centuries. Benedikt envisioned Him so clearly as He rode into the glorious, sun-drenched city, whose walls and buildings, along with Jesus riding the ass, he had seen illustrated in a Bible history. The branches that people cut from the trees and threw before the ass's hooves were shaped like frost roses on a windowpane, but they weren't white, that he knew well. They were green, lushly green, and with something of the sun stored in their smooth leaves. And suddenly the words of the old book carried almost audibly through the air, as if the waves of the ether had preserved them and all you had to do was lend them an ear: 'Behold, thy King cometh unto thee, meek, and sitting upon an ass, and a colt the foal of an ass.'

Meek, yes. Benedikt understood that. How could the Son of God be otherwise? And riding on the foal of an ass, a beast of burden – for of all that is living or dead, there is nothing too humble for service, nothing that is not sanctified by service. And only by service. Even the Son of God. Only by service. And just then, it seemed to Benedikt as if he knew the little ass and realised fully how it and the Son of God felt at that holy hour. And in his mind, he vividly saw people spreading their best garments on the road, and he heard others asking: Who is this? Imagine that: who is this! For they did not know the Son of God. Yet they ought to have known Him. A smile shone on His deeply simple face, which was dimmed just a little by sadness at how they knew no better, that their eyes were so clouded, the mirror of their hearts so fogged. And at the sight of that sorrowful smile, Benedikt's temper flared: how blind they must have been, to stand face to face with the Saviour and not recognise Him! He himself would have recognised Him immediately, at first glance — of that he was convinced. And he would have joined Him straightaway and helped Him to drive out those insolent villains from the temple and overturn the tables of the money changers and the seats of those who sold doves.

At these thoughts, Benedikt loosened his leather cap, wiped his forehead. Walking wasn't particularly strenuous for him, but these pugnacious thoughts made him sweat. He was a peaceful man; it had never so much as crossed his mind, at least not since he became an adult, to use violence against others. But at the Saviour's words — 'My house shall be called the house of prayer, but ye have made it a den of thieves' — at these words, a burning indignation kindled in him. Just imagine if the merchant decided to move his humbug store into their old turf church. There would be no peace. And with these words of the Saviour in his ear, he felt ready for whatever might come, under the Lord's guidance. Money changers, certainly. Dove sellers, yes indeed. Hucksters in general! He knew who they were. Best to think as little as possible about them. Again he wiped his forehead. And as for the hucksters he knew, the merchant and a few hawkers, he actually – despite whatever criticism they had coming – didn't relish the idea of having to give them a taste of his fists.

Thus did Benedikt walk and think and have his joys and his worries, while the grey day gradually darkened around him and the full moon lit up behind the clouds and sometimes gave a glimpse of itself against the dim evening sky. He didn't give too much thought to himself, did Benedikt, as he marched on. How could he? To the eye, now that the day was dwindling, he was gradually becoming only an indistinct shadow in the landscape. And yet, you could ask whether his self-image wasn't even more indistinct and blurred. After all, he was only a farmhand, a labourer, and had been all his life. Or perhaps more correctly: half-farmhand, half-smallholder. There was, in fact, something incomplete and insignificant about him. Half-good, half-bad, half-human, half-beast. Ah, yes – it was no different than that! In the summer, he worked as a day labourer on the farm where he lived year-round. In the winter, he looked after the sheep there in exchange for board and some clothing. Only for brief periods in spring and autumn, along with the time that he spent on his Yuletide mountain trek, was he his own master. In addition, he had an outbuilding that was his own, a stable and barn for his horse, his sheep and his hay, which he mowed on rented meadows on Sundays after church. So, he had it good, and was of course just a simple man and servant, not expecting or aspiring to be anything else, not even in the Kingdom of Heaven – not any more. Those times were past. The days and nights when he dreamed dreams and harboured longings for happiness and leisure in this life and the next. Past, yes, and it was a good thing, too! Only then had he felt unfree. Since then, he had become a little more human – since then, yes, he had become human. Unless that was also vanity and reprehensible arrogance?

But in any case, he was already an old man, fifty-three, meaning he probably wouldn't be going astray on too many long, wild roads hereafter. Fifty-three years – and it's the twenty-seventh time he's made this trip. He knows this precisely, keeps track of the number from year to year. The twenty-seventh time. He was twenty-seven years old when he started making these expeditions. Twenty-seven times he has traversed the settlement, setting out most often on Advent Sunday itself – as today. Oh, how time flies. Twenty-seven years . . . So deep did the dreams lie hidden. *Those* dreams. Which only he and God Almighty knew. And the mountains, to which he had cried out his dreams in despair. On his very first trip, he had left them there, where they lay well kept. Or perhaps they weren't so well kept after all? Did they haunt the solitude of the mountains, like exiled spirits living their fugitive, distorted lives in a desert of snow and weathered rock? Was it in fact them that he had to go check on every winter, to see if they hadn't yet faded and sunk into the earth? But he shook these thoughts off. No, he wasn't that pathetic.

But now they were approaching their stopping place for the night and were trudging up the slope that led to the farmyard, Benedikt, Eitill and Leó. The farm buildings stood on a small stretch of hills surrounded in a semicircle by the slopes of the heath behind it. This was especially beneficial in the spring, when the sun gained strength, yet at the same time the buildings were nicely sheltered. Benedikt drew a single deep breath now that he had reached the end of the road for today, then turned and looked back at the path he had travelled. He had taken hold of one of Eitill's horns, which felt warm at the base, and on the other side of him was Leó, wagging his tail. There they stood. It was something of a solemn moment. It was not as if Benedikt felt the heavens open above him, yet there was something of a rift in them; he wasn't alone on earth, didn't feel completely abandoned. Not completely abandoned, no. They stood there, and Benedikt looked out over the land and took in what he saw. Cool twilight descended over the high countryside as the day waned and the moon began to shine dimly from a sky where icy peaks drifted, peaks that appeared quite as real as the horizon's fading mountain ranges with their dull contours of snow. The farmland looked flatter on an evening like this, when the lake was frozen over and the ice was covered in snow. And in the midst of that freezing world, which now merged with the dissolution into darkness, and as a part of that dim evening, stood the man, half-farmhand, half-smallholder. He stood there with his closest friends, the wether Eitill and the dog Leó – and that world was his. Here, he lived, as a part of all that he could reach and grasp with his sight and hand and thought and insight. This world was his. Of this life, he was a part.

Not that he thought of it in that way, not consciously. He didn't even think once about how he had stopped here and stood looking out, because he usually set off from Botn before it grew light in the morning and was already high up in the mountains when day broke. He just had a kind of emptiness in his chest, a feeling of something lacking that couldn't be pinned down or clarified – a strange, draining homesickness, but whether it was because he had to leave the settlement for a few days or because, when parting from it, he was always assailed by a reminder that in a while he would have to leave it forever, he didn't know. For a man clings to his things, clings to himself and his things beyond death, fearful of losing his life – this most real of all that is real, this most fragile of all that is fragile, this most infinite of all that is infinite – fearful that it will slip from his grasp. He fears the loneliness that determines his self and *is* his self, fears being without his fellow humans around him, perhaps forgotten by God. It's a small comfort to think that he'll be buried here, if all goes well, and will remain firmly anchored in the earth. And he hopes that from the beyond, he'll have, when time allows, a view of his home district; anything else could hardly be conceivable.

As he stood there now, Benedikt couldn't help but snort disgruntledly at a few snowflakes, a few lost, softly falling snowflakes, which seemed to have no business being there, and to which he'd never before thought to pay any attention, either.

He wasn't entirely satisfied with the weather outlook, he had to admit. It honestly appeared as if he could expect, well, a bit of everything. He sniffed in the direction of the moon. Maybe snow, in fact. If not something worse. Eitill had been so sullen today, after all! And he definitely knew a thing or two. Only Leó faced the future with canine light-heartedness, curled his tail excitedly, struck out on visits and adventures of every type and couldn't have asked for better. There were times when Benedikt nearly lost patience with him – that pope-injay! But then he thought better of it and gave Leó's ear a friendly tug: Old fellow. Yet he couldn't shake off his restlessness; neither heaven nor earth held any solace for him as he stood there in the dwindling day and could no longer placate himself by plodding through heavy snow and toiling onwards. The portents of foul weather that he carried in his blood were impossible to shout down. Should he have stayed home? His rucksack suddenly felt so heavy. He laid it on the tethering stone and turned towards the door. But he didn't have to knock – he couldn't recall ever having had to here at Botn, at least not on Advent Sunday – for just then, the front door opened to reveal Sigríður, the housewife, who stepped out.

Greetings and salutations, said Benedikt, and his cold, bony hand closed around her fingers, which bore the home's warmth.

Bless you and welcome, replied the housewife. Looking from the corner of her eye at the drifting clouds, she changed her tone and said jokingly: You know, we'd been half-hoping you wouldn't turn up.

Indeed, said Benedikt. And after a moment: Well, I've already laid aside my things. Hopefully you won't deny me shelter for the night?

This was also supposed to be a joke, but its tone let it down. It sounded forced, and exposed what it should have concealed. To remedy that,

Benedikt began uninvited to scrape the snow from his shoes. In the meantime, Leó greeted the housewife, probably remembering the previous nights he'd stayed here at Botn, and then started to exchange dog news with the dogs who lived there. The housewife went and scratched Eitill behind the ear, which Eitill put up with, but coolly.

Then she laughed: He's never been downright cheerful, your Eitill, but I've rarely seen him so moody!

Benedikt mumbled something.

Is it the weather? asked Sigríður. Something in her manner contradicted her cheerful tone.

Benedikt said little in response as he stood there, bent forwards, scraping off snow; he mumbled something else, of which only the last words were completely audible: He is, you know, one of the *great* prophets.

You can almost see it in him! said the farmwife.

No, not like that, replied Benedikt, defending his Eitill. He is in reality; it's not at all imaginary, if that's what you mean.

But now Pétur, the man of the house, came along at his leisure — a little later than his wife, as was usual on Advent Sunday here at Botn.

And immediately after him came their eldest son, Benedikt. Behind him appeared a group of children, who were immediately shooed back into the house. The evening was too cold.

In with you and close the door! Benedikt will be right behind you.

Benedikt greeted the father and son, looking them in the eye for a moment as he shook their hands. He had a particular way of greeting them. After all, the son was his especially good friend, perhaps the only one. How it came about that he was named Benedikt, no one knew. The name didn't occur in either Pétur's or Sigríður's family, nor was it common in this part of the country. Hereabouts, there were only two people called Benedikt.

Of course, you'll be wanting first to put Eitill under a roof, said the farmer, standing neighbourly beside the wether. Being tactful and an expert on sheep, he was careful not to touch him, although his fingers itched to do so. And how was it again? Wasn't there something about his wanting neither water nor hay unless you fed it to him by hand?

Well, it's not quite that bad, said Benedikt, to excuse his Eitill. But he's a polite animal – apart from the fact that he has his quirks, of course. Come here, Eitill!

Meanwhile, the housewife had gone back to her tasks. Out of the door wafted the promising smells of smoked lamb and coffee and crêpes. But the three men were in no hurry; with the wether at their heels, they sauntered towards an outbuilding, in which a guest room was prepared for Eitill from year to year, a partitioned-off corner of the sheep shed where the wether had water and a manger and a resting place for himself, without being thronged or having to feed in competition with less heroic fellow creatures but still having suitable company. The water had been brought there in good time to take off its chill, and now the manger was filled with fresh, fragrant hay.

Eitill dipped his muzzle decorously into the water and quenched his thirst, then thoughtfully helped himself to the good fodder.

Pétur looked at him, then at Benedikt: So, you find the weather suitable for excursions in the mountains, you two?

You'll have to ask Eitill about that, said Benedikt, brushing aside the question. All I have is human understanding.

Which is not bad, as long as it's used with diligence, said Pétur, who'd perhaps already asked Eitill and received an answer; perhaps the previous had been put as a question more for the sake of politeness. No more was said. They barred the door carefully and walked sedately back to the farmhouse in the uncertain moonlight, which could hardly be called light, bordering as it did on darkness. Suddenly, from out of the opaque night, cold gusts of wind swept strangely and menacingly around them. People who walk together in darkness disappear from each other in such a peculiar way. Yet that isolation in darkness is different from the isolation you feel in the mountains. Down here among the farms it isn't so absolute; you can hear voices other than your own, feel nearby breaths. The profound desolation of outer space and the stony depths doesn't chill you to the roots of your hair.

Waiting for them inside the farmhouse door stood a candle, which had been burning there alone for some time. A solitary candle is almost like a person, almost as abandoned as a doubting soul, and changes so peculiarly once it's no longer alone, once people turn up. As this candle did now: as soon as the three men stepped through the door, it no longer stood there so lonely and forlorn; it suddenly had a service to perform, a duty to fulfil. Benedikt took his rucksack, which he'd put down on the tethering stone, and hung it on a nail behind the door. A chock-full sack of hay stood ready, leaning against a post.

Benedikt sniffed the hay, lifted the sack: You thought more about Eitill's belly than my old back when you filled this!

The farmer chuckled, and as they went in, he pinched the candle's wick between two fingers. It's most merciful to a candle not to allow it to languish uselessly, but rather, to revive it on occasion to a life of service – and this, of course, is most thrifty as well.

They went to the family room and there met the housewife and group of children, and the Benedikt who was a guest in the house had food set for him on a table leaf under the gable window: smoked meat straight out of the pot with potatoes in white sauce – good food for cold days, real Christmas food.

You would think I was being sent out into the wastelands, said Benedikt, who didn't feel the mountains to be a wasteland – after all, he was going there now for the twenty-seventh time. He didn't say it, didn't mention anything about this being an anniversary, a kind of jubilee, but it kept popping up in his thoughts like a refrain: the twenty-seventh time.

Well now – once you leave Botn it's usually a while before you taste warm food again, said the housewife, solicitous of her guest, making sure that he ate his fill. Now, eat! Leó has been taken care of.

When his name was mentioned, Leó looked up from the corner of the room where he lay curled up, not unlike a snail's shell, a black and white dog with yellow spots, and wagged his tail amicably at the large creatures who remembered him and were able to appreciate him even when he slept. Then he eagerly curled up again and went back to sleep, taking the opportunity while he had it.

And now as they sat making small talk, they heard a knocking on the door, three times – presumably meaning visitors for the night, although it was well known in the settlement that visitors apart from Benedikt weren't altogether welcome at Botn on Advent Sunday. They sat quietly for a moment, then young Benedikt got up and went to open the door.

It's likely the folk from Grímsdalur, reckoning they can accompany you to the mountain hut – their wethers are still out in the meadows along the Jökulsá River, said Pétur. And now he left the room, too.

I doubt they only want your company, heading up there – they're probably thinking that you could help them gather the wethers, you and Leó and Eitill! said the housewife, irritated. She couldn't suffer people imposing on others, sponging off their strength and goodwill. Why couldn't they leave Benedikt alone to go about his business?

You just go your own way, and see to it that you finish up while there's still food in your box, you promise me that, she insisted, serving him another helping of meat and potatoes, which had been prepared specifically for him; she would see what she could rustle up for the others.

But however reluctant Benedikt was to refuse anyone anything, least of all Sigríður at Botn, he couldn't promise this. He knew himself too well for that. So, he just ate and kept quiet.

If they're late, they'll just have to pay the

consequences, the housewife continued. If you start wasting time helping them gather their sheep, you'll easily squander a couple of days.

Well, there's squandering and then there's squandering, Benedikt replied, slowly and thoughtfully.

He would rather not get into a long discussion of such an irremediable thing. For if there was someone who needed to gather his sheep and he and Leó and Eitill were at hand and could help, and were perhaps even indispensable for the task, what other choice did he have but to join forces with that person? He sighed a little at these new and unforeseen inconveniences, but that's just how it was, like that and no different.

It will make a big dent in your provisions, Sigríður continued. She wasn't unaccustomed to his stubbornness and obstinacy and intransigence when it came to looking after himself, using his common sense.

Now, now, I'm well provided for, replied Benedikt unconcernedly.

You're an impossible person, that's what you are.

But now the strangers came down the

passageway, and sure enough, it was Hákon from Grímsdalur and his two farmhands. They didn't exactly seem surprised to see Benedikt, but said something like: Oh yes, it's around this time that you usually head up there and delouse old Stremba! We should have remembered that because it's a high holiday, for sure, as certain as any other, that is to say here at Botn and for old Stremba, who's otherwise unused to wintertime visitors.

Stremba – the tough one – was the name people used for the region's common highland pastures between the glacier tongues. The herdsmen found the place difficult to traverse and were loath to go there.

I dare say it's the weather that has tempted you others to set out today of all days, Sigríður remarked, a little pointedly.

Just listen to the housewife! laughed Hákon from Grímsdalur. Tempted? Come, come. Forced, good mistress – forced! A farmer with sheep grazing on mountain pastures late in the autumn can't be too fussy or discreet in his dealings with his neighbour. Besides, we can help our Benedikt a little on his hike up tomorrow; he has a good deal to carry and we're strapping fellows, aren't we, lads? Otherwise, I'd be seriously mistaken if we didn't get a tailwind up over the slopes – and that with a vengeance!

Very likely, Benedikt said quietly. Well, any weather is better with us than against us. In the mountains.

Going with you and Leó and Eitill (he didn't say the Trinity, although it was obvious that he was thinking it), we at least have hope of making it to the hut and saving our lives, Hákon joked. Whatever happens with the wethers!

You should have brought them home at least a week ago, Benedikt said placidly, without a hint of reproach; he simply stated this fact.

Should have, could have, good Bense, chuckled Hákon from Grímsdalur. Ah, yes – should have, could have!

But Benedikt didn't hear him. He had turned his ear to something else: Am I hearing wrong?

But he didn't hear wrong. A gale was already scouring the frozen roofs, a lashing, howling blizzard like a host of wild beings unleashed out there in the night. In a small room under a turf roof, surrounded by dark night, you don't think of the weather as a lifeless thing, hearing it raging like that. Winter, a formless creature, but alive and kicking – alive to the point of wildness and fury – has returned and you can hear that it feels at home. Oh yes, Eitill, as usual, had known – known far too well what was in the offing. Benedikt yanked himself to his feet; now he wanted to sleep.

Now the stray sheep in the mountains would surely be buried in snow, covered over by a snowy winter blanket before he could find them and bring them home. Because you really couldn't hope that they would have the sense to seek the heights – the heights, where the wind blew hardest, but which were their only salvation when earth and sky stand as one. When wildness rages, you hardly dare hope. And if they had indeed headed to the heights, they may just as well have frozen to death! But now he wanted to sleep. Or just lie there alone. A person shouldn't share his anxieties with others. Everyone has enough of their own.

And now they slept in the farmhouse's small family room, where heath and mountains met. And outside, the storm raged, raged and razed; many a storm raged around the world, many things happened. For this was just a small recess of the world. Here, practically only the sky raged; here it was so peaceful. Otherwise, moss and lichen grew here on the rocks under meagre conditions, that life by which the Creator transforms the stone over millennia into soil, the stone that is spewed out from the craters – and transforms the earth's fire into growth and crops, on which dew settles at midsummer and frost in the autumn nights. It's good for a person to sleep now and then.

But, as Hákon from Grímsdalur said the next morning, Sunday's smoke is Monday's flame!

There really wasn't much more to say about this Monday. At Botn, only the children welcomed the blizzard; they were over the moon, because now Benedikt was forced to stay put. And Benedikt took it good-naturedly and divided his day between Eitill and the children. When he wasn't out tending to Eitill, which in such weather required preparation and took time, he sat with the children gathered around him and carved animals and birds, carved people, made various gadgets out of sticks and carved ships with masts and bowsprits and rudders and a dinghy to hang in the stern, and all the while he told them fairytales and fish stories.

Hákon and his men stuck to card games and now and then shored up their spirits with a dram of schnapps, both of these things helping to nourish and fortify the heart. Or so Hákon claimed: They nourish and fortify the heart, yes!

For his heart was a little uneasy about the wethers along the Jökulsá River, but only a little; fate has its ways, and good things come to those who wait – that was his experience. And in between, he read newspapers and became absorbed in what he read. Because in foreign countries it was people, not livestock, who froze to death! That's how backwards things were. Bense would really have his hands full there! And they don't just freeze to death, they die and kick the bucket like flies, perish from hunger and misery. Even in the summer, in nothing but sunshine! You would think it was a lie if it didn't stand there in print.

So, for all that, said Hákon, I give thanks and praise for Stremba and our piece of the world! And many hundreds of thousands more people than live on the whole of Iceland with its surrounding islands and skerries are unemployed out there in the big countries and dawdle the hours away with nothing to do. Now, why that would be so terrible, we can't really understand here, where many a man would willingly take their place – isn't that so, lads? So don't come and tell me that it's all some big cock-and-bull story and the newspapers aren't worth the paper they're printed on. Especially the ones we read for free. And to keep you from falling into idleness and unemployment, like abroad: Come, lads! Let's play another little round. And you still don't want to join us, Bense? Right then, we'll go on with widow whist!

Widow whist. Ah, yes, Benedikt had known that game for some years – twenty-seven years – but had never played it with variously coloured cards. And so passed that day.

Tuesday morning, Benedikt was up early. A good, strong wind still blew, but the weather had settled a shade. It wasn't quite as abysmally snowy as the day before, and besides, you got used to it. He stood there in the darkness and turned his cheeks, still warm from the night, towards the snowstorm, first one, then the other. The snow had stopped coming down, he could tell, and was only drifting, which could of course be maddening enough to deal with. But it wasn't unthinkable that it might decide to subside later in the day, in which case it would be good to be on his way into the mountains, having put part of the route behind him. So, he hurried in and woke the Grímsdalur men. He was leaving now – were they coming with him?

I'd rather not, answered Hákon, getting out of bed to listen to the weather, sniff it, taste it. I'd certainly rather not – I'd rather bloody not!

Benedikt simply prepared to leave. It was his business, Hákon's, whether he wanted to go with him or not.

Will you take responsibility? asked the Grímsdalur farmer.

For Eitill and Leó and myself, yes, answered Benedikt.

Haste makes waste, said Hákon, and, with a curse word or two, made ready to follow him. But even if you won't take responsibility for us, I'm sure you'll let my lads carry the hay sack! Right then – Pétur and Sigríður, thank you for everything! And let's hope that we make it back alive. Otherwise, we'll just be even more of an annoyance to you. Don't forget the deck of cards, lads!

From the front of his rucksack, Benedikt drew a small blanket, which he laid over Eitill's back to prevent the snow from settling into his wool and weighing him down during their wanderings.

The Grímsdalur farmer asked whether the pope shouldn't also wear a chasuble.

Letting him talk, Benedikt hitched a line to Eitill's horn – come then!

Eitill was unwilling and made no secret of it. And Hákon, for his part, made no secret of the fact that he found Eitill wiser than his master. But here it was Benedikt who decided. And so they set out.

When Eitill saw that this was serious and that they wouldn't bend to him, he was willing enough. As soon as he felt the line around his horns, he got a move on, ran along like a dog – he was determined to show Benedikt that it wasn't due to angst or unwillingness that he was reluctant to leave the house. But sweet-tempered: that he wasn't today. Leó had to watch out. If the wind caught him and blew him into Eitill or into his path, he got a taste of the wether's horns.

But Leó didn't allow himself to become either irritated or dispirited; in this as in all else he was a veritable pope. He didn't let it bother him at all, didn't bite back a single time, but stayed busy showing that he knew his business – if the others got lost in the snow, then he would lead them home.

The four men there on the move had the storm and snow blowing almost directly into their backs, fortunately. Once they had reached the verge of the slope and the flatter, undulating terrain of the plateau began, it made the walk easier. The snow's surface had been lashed to a hard crust and, because of that, could bear weight for the most part. Only Eitill, with his pointed hooves, broke through it regularly. The men had brought bottles of hot coffee with them from Botn, and they stopped to drink it in the shelter of a boulder. The darkness had slowly ebbed from the world as they toiled upwards; now it was only the dense, driving snow that hid the landscape's forms and made them feel as if they were walking in place. But they just went on walking. Putting one foot in front of the other and in the right direction, they made progress. Now and then they recognised a gravel bank, a rock, a ravine. They were on the right track. Gradually, the storm lost strength and they began glimpsing the outlines of the nearest ridges, and then of the nearest peaks – only hazily, of course.

The blowing snow under the low-hanging, woolly clouds obscured every contour, but the earth was taking shape again, stepping forth in its usual image.

There these men walked, through the short day with their dogs and the wether, walked and walked. As they walked, a night passed away to the west, and soon another one caught up with them from the east. The day was so short that they hiked it away between the mountains, almost without knowing it. It was gone. A new night closed in around them. But they just walked. There was hardly any talking. A stiff wind still blew. As they walked, though, they dipped into the cache of verses and stanzas from epic poems, hymns and songs that formed part of their provisions, humming or crooning one or the other according to their spirit and circumstances or as the weather changed. Benedikt had his own:

Stony heath, storm and snow
strengthen the leg and limber the knee.
Step from your shelter if life you would know –
stay there within it, you miss what's to see.

A homemade ditty, good to croon when it was windy and the wind would take the words, keeping them just between him and it. No, there was no risk of any of the others overhearing it. The men could have spared themselves the sporadic attempts to speak to each other as they hiked. Even if they shouted, the wind tore their words to shreds, flung them over the hills, where they flew away, pierced through by the sharp projectiles of the blowing snow. Hákon, who was beginning to feel the cold, offered the others schnapps, took a swig himself, and tried to heighten its effect with the old spectral verse:

> A barrelful tip into my hole
> amid the soil and stones,
> for a pungent and delightful dram
> thirst my very bones.

And now, as mentioned before, it was night again, night with scant glimpses of the moon behind ragged clouds. The trekkers were only shadows in the night and the snowy wastes. Did Benedikt know where they were going? The other three trusted that he did indeed know, and, deep down, their confidence in Benedikt and Leó and

Eitill – the Trinity, as they were inclined to call them – grew ever stronger. But what else could they console themselves with? Oh, alright – they shouldn't even ask, but just go, go.

> Take it slow, go at your ease,
> softly step, rush no more.
> After night comes always day,
> when powder's lit, the cannons roar.

And they went at their ease, taking it slow; one tends to do so after eighteen hours of walking. The devil with all 'roaring' was their attitude – although they really wouldn't have minded having a cannon shoot them the last stretch of the way, despite the considerable risk. But on they went, and suddenly a slight elevation appeared out of the night and blowing snow. A small wooden gable jutted strangely blind and dead and abandoned up from the drifts, as if it had sunk to the bottom of its melancholy and hopelessness. The rest of the house was surely to be found there under the snow. They had indeed found the mountain hut – hit right on it, in fact. This Benedikt was a wizard and master of all things. You wouldn't find many human shortcomings in him, but on the other hand, he did have two inhuman ones, in that he neither played cards nor drank schnapps. But now, where's the door? For what they needed now was a door.

Benedikt took his staff, the bottom of which was shaped like a shovel blade, and before long had shovelled the door free; the packed snow was cut easily into blocks, which they then pushed aside. And now they had a house – steps down to the door and a bit of a passageway. They went in, lit a candle, and a little later a hot coal fire crackled in the tiny stove.

Benedikt saw to Eitill first of all. He went to the spring for water – the hut was built near a mountain stream that never froze – and, after returning and Eitill was drinking, he took a handful of hay from the sack and shook it out, then cleaned Eitill's hooves as well as possible of snow and ice clumps and smeared them and his hocks with grease – good old Eitill!

The hut was divided into two spaces. You entered a stable and from there stepped into a small room with a bedstead – practically a castle, in a way. After providing for his wether, Benedikt went in to the others. Now that loneliness was at his doorstep, so to speak, he felt inwardly how good it was to be with other people, even if these ones could be a bit cheeky at times. The smell of coffee already permeated the place. Benedikt found a free spot by the stove, hung his wet clothes to dry, and set about picking lumps of ice from his hair and beard.

Well, here we are.

Yes, you're a gem and our saviour, Bense, said Hákon, quite genuinely. You should have a medal to wear to church and a sum of money from abroad. You've saved our lives, as I said, but what's a man without his sheep? A beggar, dear Bense, and nothing else. Such a man's words can't conjure up medals or monetary rewards – you can take it from me. And with my sheep, it's like this: God knows where they're to be found, that is, if anything's still to be found of them at all. Likely as not, they've all been blown into the river. Or have been buried in snow and suffocated. And here we sit and stuff ourselves. But what the hell, let's enjoy the coffee while it lasts. You never know what tomorrow will bring. And on the other hand, something so bad rarely happens that you can't imagine something even worse.

They filled their mugs and sat down, the farmer and Benedikt on the edge of the bedstead, the farmhands on the floor. And now Benedikt took his food from his rucksack and they ate bread and butter and meat and washed it down with piping-hot coffee, and it was all so good, warming them to their toes and fingertips, that they topped it off with a mountain song:

> Let's ride, lads, ride,
> drive them o'er the sands!

Ah, yes, said Hákon, if we'd been straddling nags today, our legs would have been less stiff, but on the other hand, we may have wound up stuck to our necks in a snowdrift out there somewhere.

But it was sleep and not song they needed, and by the second verse they were yawning. And now they lay down and slept.

So there they lay, sprawled on the floor, four sleeping men in a mountain hut buried in snow, four dead-tired men, whose breathing gave way continually to snores, dwindled, then struck up again, varying in strength like the storm they'd just escaped. The dogs snored, too, and even the wether Eitill made sleeping sounds. And meanwhile, high above the roof and behind the snow clouds, the constellations moved slowly by and measured out day and night – even for this little piece of earth and the creatures sleeping dead-heavily in the little hut – finished the night bang on time and let a new day dawn. And there it was. It was time to wake up to it. And they woke up – something or other called to them. Stiff and sore, they stretched life into their tired bodies, feeling as if they'd fallen asleep only a moment ago, although it was already growing light in the cabin – let's put the kettle on!

As was to be expected, it wasn't so simple finding the Grímsdalur wethers and gathering them. The storm had driven some of them away from the meadows along the Jökulsá River. First of all, it was a matter of locating them, and when they'd finally done that, they still had the difficult task of pushing through the drifts, and the days were short. They're so short around the winter solstice. Had they not had Eitill to take out to the scattered groups, which he would lead back to the mountain hut, Eitill who always kept going until he got stuck in the snow and had to be dug out, and who incessantly imparted to the others his courage and strength, how would it have gone?

What would they have done then? Hákon admitted this willingly and spared no praise for Eitill. Nor did Leó miss out on the praise, being so skilled at following even older tracks and sniffing out the sheep's hiding places, even smelling where they lay snowbound in ditches and hollows – might Benedikt consider selling him? But Benedikt would not consider selling him. Oh, no, you don't go dragging a pope to market as if it were nothing. And in the evenings they sat comfortably in the hut, and only reluctantly did without Benedikt for the communal pastime.

Still no game of cards? Well, then we'll play widow whist.

One day, two days, three days passed. The storm had subsided. The weather was calm and relatively mild, while it lasted. And then finally on Friday, a little after midday, the Grímsdalur farmer was able to set out for home with his wethers, northwards toward the settlement. They had been found and gathered, each and every one. Benedikt showed the men the way over the heath, which sloped slightly downwards toward the riverbed, received their thanks – three handshakes and a couple of nods, a few shouted farewells – then stood there for a while and watched the departees before lumbering back to the hut and closing the door. He provided the weary Eitill with water and food, patted Leó, lay down flat on his back in the empty bedstead, with one hand outside it resting on Leó, his friend, his comrade – now he wanted to rest. To be alone and just rest. To gather himself and just be completely and utterly alone, even inwardly. Advent . . . how distant last Sunday already was.

People have many different ways of living their lives. Some talk; others remain silent. Some need to be closely surrounded by their fellow human beings in order to feel good; others feel as if they're not quite themselves unless they're entirely alone, at least now and then. Generally, Benedikt wasn't shy. But on his Advent treks he'd got used to having no human company. Idle chatter and gossip from the settlement, day in, day out, here in the mountains wearied him beyond belief – it didn't belong here. It hadn't been quite so bad in his younger days. He could feel that he was growing old. Where were the peace and deep calm of last Sunday? Where was the expectation? The consolation? Was it really only five nights ago? Wait – what did he say? Was it really five nights ago!

Because, in that case, he should have been home again soon – if everything had gone according to plan. Yet here he lay, worn out like his own old clothes. And in tatters inside, too. Ah, yes, time flies; he isn't young anymore.

Had he been asleep and dreaming? Or was there a knock on the door? He must have been asleep, because Leó was at the door barking like mad, but he hadn't dreamed it, because now the knocking came again, three measured blows; Benedikt got to his feet quickly and opened the door. It was a young man from down in the settlement: Jón from Fjall.

Have you seen a group of young horses around here? he asked.

Benedikt had seen horse tracks, sure enough, particularly along the river, but also in other places. He hadn't seen the horses, though – at least they weren't here in the immediate vicinity. To tell the truth, he hadn't paid the tracks any attention; it would never have entered his head that anyone had colts in these parts at this time of year.

Does your master think you're old enough and experienced enough to be out on your own up here in the dead of winter, my boy?

Jón from Fjall insisted that whatever others could handle, he could handle too. He may be right, thought Benedikt, but nonetheless, he was young and definitely unseasoned. And now that the two of them had chanced upon each other, Benedikt felt a certain responsibility for the lad. If he, Benedikt, went on his way tomorrow without giving his attention to Jón and his horses, and then came home to the village in a few days to find that Jón hadn't returned, was still in the mountains – what then? Besides, Eitill could really benefit from a day's rest.

Let's see in the morning, he said, having already prepared coffee for the young man.

Do you mean you might find some time for us to look around a bit? asked Jón, incapable as he was of disingenuity, of having anything resembling an ulterior motive.

Time . . . what's a little time? answered Benedikt. In a way, the boy's question made him feel good. But in another way, it stung a little that the young man had evidently not reckoned on his help.

Saturday was spent looking for the horses. And they found them. On Sunday morning, the young man set off for home, bearing greetings for the settlement.

Everyone will see that even if I haven't got any farther, the week wasn't wasted! said Benedikt, who felt that a few words of explanation were necessary.

And now he was going to make the most of the day and head inwards, where no roads or paths led from one settlement to another. But he felt a bit weak in his limbs, not exactly fit for big undertakings. It had been a trying week; there was no denying it. And yet it was only child's play compared with what lay ahead.

It was quite strange to think that on this day in previous years he had sometimes been back already, been home again, over and done with everything; the sheep had been saved, and he'd sat with his heart full of gratitude and solemnity at home in the little church, listening to the priest preach about the widow's offering. Or about signs in the sun and moon – because 'there shall be signs in the sun, and in the moon, and in the stars; and upon the earth distress of nations, with perplexity; the sea and the waves roaring.' So it was written.

He, too, had once feared death, yes, and life

also, for that matter. Not least life, perhaps. Feared it, yes. But that was a long time ago. And that fear, too, lay hidden in the mountains. Now, most often, it's so quiet both inside him and around him. As quiet as in the mountains.

He sat there packing his rucksack, lost in thought. He had better shake off his fatigue and heaviness and use the day to press on farther inwards – at least part of the way. In the middle of his preparations, he got up and went out to take a look at the weather – and what was that on the other side of the river? Horses and men, indeed. It had to be the postman, being ferried over. And then what? There was no sign of anyone with horses to meet him on this side. Benedikt went quickly back in, put water on for coffee.

But the postman wouldn't stop; he had a sledge and a helper to pull it: The day is short, good Bense, and my horses are overdue and probably stuck somewhere; we must hurry in and meet them.

On the opposite bank of the river was the postman's guide, already on his way south again. Grímur from Jökull, the ferryman, had joined Benedikt, and they stood and watched those far-faring and strangely fleeting people moving off to the north and south. Grímur had nothing against a cup of coffee now that it was made; a person shouldn't scorn God's gifts.

And you seem to have settled in here for the rest of your life – both keeping house and running an inn, he joked. It's going on a week now that I've seen smoke from here. And he slung a sack of coal that he had brought with him down next to the stove. I thought you might be pretty close to the bottom of your supply, so I brought this sack. I'm the one who's supposed to be keeping that fire-gob fed, anyway. But what exactly are you doing here?

Benedikt told him that he was actually out on his usual winter ramble, but then it had gone like this and like that, and in the meantime the days came and went, and you couldn't get a great many things done in one day, particularly at this time of year.

Well done on Hákon's part, Grímur remarked. Not to mention those from Fjall!

Well, sheep and horses will always be sheep and horses, Benedikt objected, irrefutably. You have to take care of the one and not neglect the other. What good is it for me to find a few stray hooves if whole herds are lost? Hákon found his, at last, but had Leó and I not joined the search, and especially Leó . . . No, Grímur! And besides, you yourself would have done exactly as I did.

The devil I would!

Oh, please. And the good thing about it is that now I don't have to search where we've already been.

And I imagine you had to take a chunk out of your own tack, too? asked Grímur, who wasn't in agreement with him on a number of things.

Well – I generally bring enough food for half a month or more, and Hákon knew that. They carried Eitill's sack for me all the way from Botn up here.

But Grímur just shook his head, slurped his coffee fiercely from the saucer, and sucked violently on his lump of rock candy. You look dog-tired – to tell it like it is. And, dare I ask, what sort of treatment is this of Eitill? Many have been reported to the Animal Welfare Association for less, I would like you to know. He just runs until he drops, like certain others, as well you know. Aren't you responsible for him? Now we'll tie the hay sack here to a post, like this; Eitill is as sensible as a human being and will tend properly to his own needs, and we'll just make sure he has plenty of water and bedding – there now! – and now a few days of being alone won't do him any harm. Because, as I'm sure you're aware, you're not getting out of going home with me and sleeping over for a couple of nights. You can fill a sack for Eitill while you're there and bring it back here with you. And there won't be any of this digging into your own tack. No more chatter now. We've already had enough cursing here, considering we're only in the seventh week of winter and today is the feast of the Immaculate Conception.

To be rowed over a heavy-currented glacial river – after first having to drag the boat upstream a good distance, and then, while rowing across, drifting downstream several times the width of the river – is like coming to another country, almost another life. Something snaps inside you: how do I get back? But Benedikt was too tired. On the way to the ferryman's farmhouse, which lay hidden behind some hills for shelter from the worst northerly gales, he staggered from drowsiness and nearly fell asleep as he walked. In the farmyard he turned and looked back, but the mountain hut and everything in it were gone, hidden by the hills; only the northern mountains still stood in their places, but were now somehow so unreachable that it hurt him inside. Because that was where he should have been.

He had barely finished undressing when he fell asleep. And now he was in among his mountains, and found sheep and struggled with them, slogged and slogged, and for a moment Leó and Eitill were there, but in between they were gone and he was all alone with a flock of sheep, some of which were lazy, others unruly, and the storm roiled around him and brought the worst imaginable, the snowdrifts loose and bottomless, and nearby walked a man, invisible, and not just due to the weather, a man who was at once friendly and hostile to him – what did he want from him? And behind the dream he knew that time went by, that it did not stand still, did not allow itself to be stopped by rivers, never grew weary, that it flowed onwards, enigmatic as a glacial river; it passes over a sleeping man as over one dead.

Benedikt lay awake in a moonlit family room; so it was night. He felt rested. But suddenly he was restless. He jumped out of bed and woke a young farmhand in the bed opposite by gently shaking his shoulder; they sat there facing each other and dressed themselves in the moonlight, as silently as possible, then crept in their stocking feet down the stairs. They mustn't wake anyone else. The farmhand wanted to make coffee – but Benedikt asked him not to.

Wait and have a cup when you're home again; you can be back in an hour. Come now.

They whispered like a pair of conspirators, despite having already left the house. Benedikt pressed impatiently onwards: The moon is in a hurry, you see, and tonight I feel like racing it for a stretch. I can be halfway to the other hut before daybreak, and reach it by evening.

Which hut? asked the young man, who wasn't fully awake yet.

Oh – my hole up there, said Benedikt.

The hay sack stood ready behind the storehouse door; the young man tied it onto his back. If the household had been awake, Benedikt would probably have had his provisions supplemented, but so be it. In such moonlight you could almost live off the air, so he would manage: stony heath, storm and snow.

They strapped on their skis and glided in the moonlight across the ice-grey land. So high up in the mountains, every direction is only farther inwards, toward an unknown point: the core that recedes continuously while remaining still, and which was their ultimate destination. Soon the hills sloped down towards the riverbed. They made quick progress, Leó darting like an arrow past them, yapping with pleasure.

And then they were over the river. Benedikt helped to pull the boat up along the bank, then hoisted the hay sack to his neck, gave the boat a shove. Thanks and safe crossing, and give my regards to your family!

And there in the grey light and gleam of the moon, that shell of a boat glided downriver at enough of an angle to hit the opposite bank in the right place. Once more, Benedikt was alone in his land. And now he went and called on Eitill. And there in the night and the loneliness and the moonlight, a trace of holiness returned, of Advent, a remnant of notes in the air, the ringing of bells, memories of sunshine and the fragrance of hay, the hope of a summerland – or what? Perhaps it was just a distinctive sort of inner peace.

Eitill greeted the other two with a satisfied bleat, stood up, shook himself and was ready. He pressed himself up against Benedikt as the man greeted him properly and looked to see how he had got on. Yes, he even condescended to sniff back when Leó stuck his snout toward him, and Leó, honoured and delighted, wagged his tail but couldn't leave it at that, instead giving his comrade a kiss and even putting his forepaws on Eitill's back, and getting a poke from his horns, in return – given in all friendliness, of course, but a warning nonetheless. It didn't bother Leó.

Benedikt was satisfied in all respects with his Eitill, with the way he'd behaved, having eaten from the hay sack with good sense and moderation. Now the wether ate his morning hay, properly shaken out, from the manger, a clean manger. Then his water bucket was rinsed and filled with fresh water from the spring. Following that, they had a little breakfast in peace, the three of them in the hut. For the time had come.

Benedikt moved the hay sack outside and tied a line around Eitill's horn, put out the fire in the stove with water from the bucket, looked around the hut to see if everything was in order and in its place, and then went outside with his companions and closed the door. He strapped his skis on unhurriedly and hoisted his rucksack to his back, then shouldered the sack of hay, which was quite heavy at first, and walked into the moonlight with the wether on its line and his dog at his heels. It was very cold. But when the air was so still, the cold only settled like a cool breath on his skin, and didn't bite through. They took it easy, the three of them: Take it slow, go at your ease, softly step, rush no more . . . one walks so well in moonlight between mountains.

Benedikt looked up at the sky. The wheel of stars had already rotated a quarter of a turn since he stuck his head out of the farmhouse door at Jökull. So swiftly does time pass, whether you follow along with it or not. It can do you good, walking with the stars, being a bit in motion like them. He walked so well here. The snow-covered mountains seemed so low and distant in the moonlight, and here and there touches of starlight glittered against the glossy-black nighttime ice. Such a walk was like a poem with rhymes and wonderful words; it remained in the blood like a poem. And just as with a poem, you might learn it by heart, so to speak – and then feel compelled to come and look here again, to make sure that all was unchanged. And so it was: alien and unattainable – yet homely and indispensable. And, finally, complete calm fell over Benedikt. A sense of security deep in his heart expanded and became all-encompassing, infallible: here he walked. He walked here.

He was like a man on the verge of drowning who suddenly thrusts his head out of the water and is saved. The air streamed into him like spring water, and he drank it in. This was his life – walking here. And because it was this that had become his life, he could now face anything – anything – and welcome it. He had no more worries – yes, one: that he couldn't really imagine who would walk here after him. But someone must come.

Because surely it wasn't the Creator's intention that when he, Benedikt, was gone, the poor animals that strayed herein and weren't found during the autumn sheep roundups should be left to their fate? It couldn't be the Creator's intention. Because even if sheep were only sheep, they were creatures with life and blood, life and blood and soul. Or maybe Eitill was a soulless creature? Or Leó? Or Faxi? Was their innocence and trust inferior to man's frail faith? Benedikt shook his head. Whoever his successor was, he could wish him nothing better than such companions. With such companions, no one could be alone in the world. Some had other things and more – presumably. But who had something better? It would be nothing but ingratitude to think that his lot in life could have been different and richer. Ingratitude and stupidity. As if better creatures were to be found on earth than his three friends. And there was something sacred and inviolable in the relationship between man and animal. One fine day he would find himself having to make the decision: a bullet for this one, a knife for the other. That was the price. Therein lay the responsibility. Having to make oneself master of not only their lives, but also their deaths, according to one's best judgement and the dictates of one's conscience. Life was no different. It hurt. Only those who'd been through it could have any notion of how much it hurt. In a way, all animals were sacrificial animals. But – wasn't all of life a sacrifice? When it was lived properly? Wasn't this the enigma? That fecundity comes from within, is self-denial? And that all life which is not at its innermost core a sacrifice, is presumptuous and leads only to death?

But we'll let this go. It's too incomprehensible, anyhow. What was certain was that the three of them walked there in the night and the moonlight between the silent mountains and had a goal. Had a goal and knew it. All three. A humble goal, to be sure, but a goal nonetheless.

The stars paled with the morning. The contours of the mountains, too, grew duller, faded into the vague dawn. And then it was day. There's always something liberating and at the same time merciless about a day, especially at the moment of its birth. And with the day, the winds wakened. For the moment, it was only a few barely perceptible puffs from several different directions, which, as if half-asleep, stirred a bit of life into what loose snow there was. But soon afterward, the wind-folk seemed to realise which way they wanted to go that day, and started driving sledges up and down the hills, rearranging the drifts. Then the last outlines disappeared, making it difficult to distinguish anything, even the transition from snow-grey land to snow-grey sky, since the clouds lurking along the horizon had drawn themselves imperceptibly upwards so that gradually, you could only discern straight overhead the last dull remnants of last night's dark blue.

Yet it came as a surprise, like something almost unfathomable it happened so abruptly, when a new and obviously rested snowstorm suddenly seethed around Benedikt and his companions. They became so thoroughly lost in it that, although they soldiered on, almost as if nothing had changed, they barely perceived themselves or each other. But they stuck together. They withstood the madness of that howling gale and the whipping snow. The snow blew so thickly that it was scarcely conceivable that the storm could handle it, that it was capable of pressing through the snowfall and playing along, that it hadn't long since been suffocated by it. For a person here, in any case, it was hardly possible to breathe. But Benedikt gulped a little air when he could and struggled onwards, holding tightly to the line, the other end of which was somewhere out there in the swirling snow-darkness, tied around Eitill's horn. Leó had to fend for himself, and that's what he did. And there they went now, the three of them, step by step and swaying to and fro in the wild gusts of wind.

Ah, yes, they trudged through the snowstorm, there was nothing else for it. And meanwhile, the day passed – though of it, nothing could be seen, but only made out as a barely perceptible light in the churning snow. Benedikt steered toward his hut, as he called it, although it was just a hole in the ground with a hatch: a pot, a kind of burrow. He dug this hole twenty-seven years ago, roughly in the middle of the area he usually searched. And for it, he'd chosen a hill that wasn't too high – reducing the danger of the hatch, weighed down with a few stones, blowing away – and on the other hand, not so low that water would run in.

Benedikt was sure that he'd kept mainly on course and was well on his way to his pot. He just walked on and hoped that the storm would subside by evening, since it had started at dawn. And that the sky would clear up a bit. Because how else would he find his hole? But the storm wouldn't subside. It paid no attention whatsoever to Benedikt and his wishes and feelings. It seemed rather preposterous that it could have the capacity to bellow like this for a whole day, so early in the winter, but it did. The little light being ground down by the maelstrom of snow grew thinner and thinner, pulverised to pure nothingness, pulverised to darkness with a vague hint of the moon behind. Snowy darkness, whirling darkness. And the fury continued, unaltered: a roaring and groaning as of giants clashing, a battle of invisible powers, ceaseless and in every direction, a possessed, tumultuous night.

Being out on such a night, miles from all roads and your fellow creatures, alone and dependent entirely on yourself in a wasteland, a bloodthirsty mountain desert, you've got to keep your mind together, leaving no cracks for the spirits of the storm, no fissures where fear, vacillation or the madness of nature can seep in. Because life and death are placed on opposite sides of the scales – and which is heavier? Here only courage can help, the unbroken and unbreakable mind. You simply deny the danger and go on. It was that simple. So simple for a man like Benedikt: stony heath, storm and snow!

Then, in the darkness, he ran smack into a boulder. And immediately afterwards, another one. So now he needed to look after his skis, to keep them from being damaged. It would be better to take them off; this wouldn't do any longer.

With that done, he took a closer look at the last boulder, felt it, first with his mittens on, then, just to be sure, with his bare fingers, almost as you feel an animal that's for sale, then stood a little and considered, sniffed to see which way was north and which was south. Aha, he recognised this rock, for sure. He'd travelled in the right direction, yes indeed – but gone just a trifle too far.

So, time to turn around and head in the right direction, ahem. And he followed that course for a while. Then he stopped abruptly, took a turn to the right, a turn to the left, and now what he jolly well needed was a bit of luck. Roaming hither and thither like that, you soon lost your sense of direction and went astray. And suddenly Benedikt became aware of a sensation beneath his feet, or something; perhaps a certain inclination in the landscape. Very slowly, he took a couple of steps, a couple of long steps, carefully measured, then thrust his staff into the snow, first here, then there. The final time, he heard a hollow sound. It was the hatch; the hut was found. He was home.

Now the shovel went to work. It didn't take long to free up the nearly horizontally lying hatch, lift it, scramble down – with the dog and the wether at his heels. The wether and Benedikt slid more than anything else down the earthen steps, and Leó hailed the noise they made with happy barking, ruff-ruff! It was more than good; it was an incredible relief to have the storm outside, finally, and no longer be out in the middle of it. Benedikt sat down for a moment on the hay sack, so overcome with fatigue that he saw sparkles of light in the darkness. It was good to sit down. Eitill, too, expressed his satisfaction, with a thoughtful bleat. But then Eitill started shaking himself out, creating a snowstorm in the little hut, as well – and giving Leó cause to complain. After which, he immediately did the same as Eitill.

But it was Benedikt, of course, who was the one responsible here, and he had not only himself, but also his friends and travelling companions to look after. He fished the stub of a tallow candle out of his rucksack and lit it. A pair of nearly indistinguishable creatures stood there in front of him in the flickering candlelight, covered so thoroughly in snow and ice that only their eyes and mouths were recognisable, besides Eitill's horns. Benedikt immediately set about freeing his fellow trekkers from the snow and icicles as best he could.

Otherwise, they would be soaked to the skin as soon as it warmed up in there, and heading out into tomorrow's hardships would be bad enough without their skin being damp and susceptible to the cold. As it happened, Eitill's mantle provided reasonable protection where it was mainly needed. Finally, Benedikt brushed the snow off himself and plucked the ice from his hair and beard and eyebrows. And now he lit his stove. Surviving in the wilderness is much easier when you can make fire and have cooking utensils and all modern conveniences. If your matches are wet, you can stick them inside your woollen shirt and dry them against your body. It's an old home remedy. And now that the stove was lit, Benedikt opened the hatch out to the riotous night and supplied himself with a couple of blocks of snow. As he melted the snow in the saucepan, he moved back and forth between constantly refilling it and shoring up the hatch, sealing its worst gaps against the wind and snow, that's it!

After providing Eitill with hay to eat and snow to slake his thirst, he grabbed the rucksack and took out some food, giving Leó a bite, too. The meat was frozen and even the bread was icy to his teeth – oh, well, soon he would have coffee. They shared the frozen food like the friends they were, he and Leó, shared it like brothers. Benedikt wanted to meet the man who lived more like a king in his castle, felt more secure amid all the world's tribulations, and what's more, had the prospect of saving some sheep from starvation in the next few days and serving his region and society and all creation.

Let me tell you, Leó – not even the pope in Rome has it better or more luxurious than you and I, or has a clearer conscience. And Leó wagged his tail and willingly believed everything his master preached to him, all the more so as every tenet was accompanied by a treat.

And Benedikt, he sat there like the lord of a manor with a piece of meat in his hand and shared it with Leó as it gradually thawed. And there was plenty of butter here, an abundance. Leó certainly didn't have to eat his bread dry. Here they sat, yes indeed – it could have gone worse, and today was Wednesday, to be sure . . .

In other words: he'd been gone for over a week. It was nine days, to be exact, since he set out from Botn, and for seven of those, he'd lived on his own provisions. Yes indeed. And it had left its mark on them; that couldn't be denied. He'd scrimped and saved as best he could, but in truth there were only seven not-too-large pieces of meat left, besides a supply of bread, which, no harm in saying, could have been more ample. But what did the Lord get out of two loaves of bread and one fish? With that, he'd fed thousands. It sounded unimaginable, but in the face of such facts, you couldn't in decency give up hope. After all, he had only himself and Leó to provide with human food. But miracle or no miracle, they had to be frugal; nowhere is prudence forbidden in the law. One piece of meat a day – that's it! No more can be spared. It also had its advantages; not being weighed down with food made him much lighter on his feet. But what was going on with the candle? What was the matter with the Primus? He pumped it, but it didn't help much. It wanted to go out, at all costs; it would settle for nothing else. And that, despite there being enough paraffin in it. What kind of witch-craft was this? Was his hole haunted? Had some ghoul crept in here to devour the light? Just then, Benedikt found himself in darkness.

And it was no natural darkness. It was a highly

unnatural darkness; it literally stung his eyes and took him by the throat, seemingly intent on suffocating him. At the same time, it was friendly enough, wanting to lull him to sleep, just sleep; let him sink away and sleep. What did he need that coffee for, anyway? Why did he want more light in the evening? But was it pure kindness, he wondered? He tried to figure it out, tried to collect himself, to think. Surely the storm wasn't after them, even now? He'd carefully sealed every crack. It must be intending to suffocate them! Of all the . . . !

Benedikt got to his feet, as difficult as it was to tear himself out of his drowsiness, staggered to the hatch and pushed it up. By then, though, he was in the grip of dreams. Outside, he'd expected to find the freedom of a starry night. But there, the same storm seethed, threatening to fill the hole in an instant. The hatch was re-shut, but in such a way that the snow could not cover it completely.

And as was to be expected, both the candle and the stove were now willing to live a little again, to continue the enterprise they'd previously abandoned. Then the coffee was ready. The smell of it filled the hut – ah, coffee! Benedikt drank it with devotion. And when it was drunk, he put out the light. It was night therein. His limbs slackened and the blood coursing through them murmured itself into tranquillity. Sleep came gliding nearer, nearer, then it was there and took him in its arms.

Benedikt lay there in his pot, his burrow, with his wool blanket wrapped around him and the hay sack under his head. He lay up close to Eitill, who was sleeping in his own way and occasionally ruminating comfortably. Leó lay down close to the other two, whimpering contentedly in anticipation of rest. There they lay, the three of them, a few feet below the ground, insignificant and scarcely reckonable as alive. Yet they had to waken the next day to exploits of which most others were incapable, undertakings that only they were able and willing to do. Were they not as inconsequential as they seemed? Were they perhaps essential components of a cohesive whole? Over them, the night advanced.

Benedikt slept like a rock. Completely gone in a bottomless night. Suddenly he was awake, abruptly as always, wide awake – and felt rested. Now it was a matter of extricating himself from the blanket and sleep before the fatigue, which was probably lurking somewhere, got hold of him again. Then he got to his feet, shoved back the hatch – moonlight! It was moonlight indeed. So the world was once more in order, more or less. And he hadn't overslept, either, unless an entire day had gone by the board – and there was nothing to be done about that. Take it slow, go at your ease.

Benedikt had saved a bit of his meat the evening before; this he now shared with Leó. Then they shared the day's allowable portion of bread. Benedikt washed his down with a couple of cups of coffee. Today, Eitill would be allowed to stay in the hole and rest, Benedikt decided. Of the three of them, he was the worst for wear following yesterday's strenuous journey. There was no good reason to inconvenience him until it was known for certain that he would be needed. If it went as it usually did, things could get pretty rough before they returned home. So, Benedikt supplied him with hay and fresh snow, melted a little snow for him so he could have a drink of water, then saw to it that there was a breathing hole next to the hatch. Leó watched with an anxious air, looked his master in the eye several times, fawned a little and lifted his paw doubtfully, unsure of whether he should start scratching the snow away again or what, but Benedikt had made up his mind entirely and just patted him on the back. Finally, Leó regained his composure when he saw that they weren't taking their provisions with them. And then they went together out into the moonlit night, Benedikt and Leó.

Since the weather was so calm and clear and he'd woken up rather early, Benedikt wanted to start by searching the most distant area, a trough valley at the foot of the glacier, five hours there and five back – in the best case. So that was what he did. He rarely ever found any sheep there, but he would never have allowed himself to return home without having checked first. Benedikt started off slowly, toiling up the hills, then swept like a gust of wind down the slopes: stony heath, storm and snow!

But the day wasn't as lucky as the weather was good. Benedikt found no sheep – none alive. At the bottom of the aforementioned valley, which was already almost entirely filled with drifts, he found only a hole in the snow in one place. As a matter of fact, it was Leó who found it, a hole dug by a fox,

and sure enough, it led down to a sheep's carcass —
he was too late!

This discovery so upset Benedikt that he was in
a foul mood the rest of the day. Because this was a
bad sign, a terrible omen. This year was supposed
to be a kind of jubilee: not just his twenty-seventh
trek — but he himself was almost twice twenty-
seven years old. Yes, it truly was a landmark year,
at least for him. But then it had to go like this.
What's more, he'd got off on the wrong foot right
from the start. And up here things weren't as they
should be, either, although there was little to
complain about as far as the weather and the conditions underfoot were concerned. The mountains
stood so strangely silent and sullen around him.
What had he done to them? Was it his fault that he
was late? Or was it because he had stopped to rest
at Jökull? That would just be petty, he felt. And in
any case, he knew he wasn't to blame. He'd come
as quickly as he possibly could, considering how
things had gone. So, if they really wanted to be
surly with him and disobliging, it was up to them!
From that moment on, he paid them no more
attention; when he looked around, it was for sheep
and only sheep. And when there were no sheep

to be seen, not even a trace of them, he clenched his teeth and — furious at the twisted mountains — hurried back to his hut and Eitill and the comfort of his pot, his burrow.

But once he reached it and had crept down into the earth and shut the hatch over him, neither his food nor even his coffee tasted any good, and he slept only a little that night, and restlessly. It isn't easy being at loggerheads with old friends — to lose, as it were, his last refuge in a lonely world. And if there is anything that can poison the blood, it's this: to find only dead sheep when you go out looking for living ones.

The next day, which was a Friday, the adventure began. Benedikt set out with the dog and the wether — the whole Trinity went on the move. A wind had arisen from the north. The snow swept so delicately up and down the hills, as if solely to ensure that Benedikt was able to move smoothly and easily, or it performed fleeting ring dances around boulders and large rocks, embracing them elfishly, with a chilly gracefulness. Despite this, it wasn't a good day to search for sheep, because in such weather, they seek shelter, and their tracks are immediately blown over. But Benedikt brushed this aside. He had to search there, no matter how intractably the weather and the mountains behaved. And his diligence was rewarded. The luck that had failed him yesterday under clear skies returned and sought him out here in the middle of the swirling snow. Quite early in the day he found two sheep, in the evening a third, and on his way home he ran into two more, so now there were five. It was almost like sinking one's net into a foggy sea, this search in drifting snow, but fortunately, he caught something. Because when you know the peculiarities of the landscape and the most favourite haunts of the sheep, and also have a dog who's a veritable pope, you find sheep even blindly. That's how it was. And now, indeed, in the midst of all the turmoil, things started gaining some clarity, seemed to be heading in the right direction, which improved his mood.

But all three of them, Benedikt, Eitill and Leó, had great difficulty with those mountain vagabonds. Each of the two pairs stuck together and wanted nothing to do with other creatures. One moment they tore off, one pair to the east, the other to the west, and then in the next they could barely be budged, but had to be driven onward with shouts and screams and the dog's barking, or downright dragged through the snowdrifts. It was hugely taxing.

This, though, was Eitill's time to shine, and he certainly lived up to his name – tough as a knot. He joined up with those unfamiliar sheep, convinced them that he, like they, had only one thought, to flee from the dog and the man, and led the way – in the right direction, of course. At times he had them well under control and got them running as a group, and all Benedikt and Leó had to do was chase after them as best they could. But then those vagrants would get other ideas in their heads, splinter and bound away and have to be gathered again. Or Eitill would get stuck in a snowdrift and be unable to free himself, with his whole retinue tailing him. Then it would be Benedikt's turn to clear a path, pulling Eitill by the horn, while Leó, at the rear, kept the tail in one piece. At times all six sheep had to be pulled through the drifts – making the herders work up a sweat. So the day went.

On that day, taking Eitill back to the hut was out of the question; he had to stay and keep the newly found sheep together, find something for them to graze on and keep them busy saving their own lives, so they wouldn't give into their whims and urges and flee. And since it would be lonely in Benedikt's pot without Eitill and they found themselves halfway between it and the mountain hut, and since today the postman was expected to be heading south again and would in all probability spend the night in the hut, Benedikt decided to head there. Then he could also entrust a message to the settlement with the postman's guide, who would take the horses northward again. He didn't want anyone at home to be worrying about him.

So there he walked and walked, out of the day and into the night, walked and walked. And made it to the hut. But he had misreckoned: at the hut he found only the postman's horses – the postman must have been ferried over the river that evening, and his guide, who was to go north again, must have gone with him. But the guide would surely return early the next morning. Or at least sometime tomorrow. Benedikt would wait for him and take that day to rest, although he had only a single scrap of frozen meat in his pocket. Surely the man from the settlement would have something by way of a refreshment to offer him. On

Sunday morning, Benedikt could head back west – it would be the third Sunday in Advent.

But it didn't work out that way; his planned day of rest came to nothing. Long before dawn on Saturday morning, Benedikt was on his way inwards again, on his way towards found and unfound sheep. It was impossible, after all, leaving Eitill in the lurch like that. But before he left, he gave the postman's horses water and hay, so that the guide could see that he'd been there and hopefully let folk in the settlement know that he was alright.

In the grey light of dawn that Saturday morning, the wind turned into a storm, again a storm, always a storm, mountain and winter weather, a real blizzard, which stood like a wall around the solitary, wandering man. He had to trudge continually through such walls, trudge through mountains of drifting snow. But somehow, in a way that was incomprehensible to him, he maintained his grasp of the landscape and directions, found Eitill with his flock of sheep unsundered, and now he trekked north again, almost directly against the storm, in the direction of the settlement, slowly, step by step and barely even that. Again it was trudging through the drifts and dragging the exhausted, recalcitrant sheep. Only Eitill followed him unreluctantly.

Then it was evening. The fight with those foolish sheep and the crazy weather had taken a heavy toll on Benedikt. What was more, hunger had begun gnawing at his belly. He'd been without food for quite some time, and before that, had been on limited rations. He had little hope of reaching his hole with the sheep before evening. The weather and the going had conspired against him, forcing him to abandon his plan, so he left the sheep with Eitill for one more night and returned alone to his hole. People are so powerless. It's of little use to kick against the goads when you're commanded by stronger powers. He still had a couple of hours to go, he estimated. And so, he walked – for a couple of hours, as far as he could tell. But there was no hut to be found, no hole, no pot, no burrow to crawl into. Well, then!

The earth can behave so adversely towards people that it closes itself off entirely from them. Then there's nothing for it but to see what can be done – and Benedikt found a way. It's humanity's task, perhaps the only one, to find a way. Never to give up. To kick against the goads, no matter how sharp they are. To kick against the very goad of death, until it pierces through and strikes the heart. This is humanity's task.

When your feet refuse to go farther, stop using them, but don't give up for that reason. They want to rest, which is only fair – let them rest. It would be good to sit down. Downcast, but not broken, Benedikt planted his staff in the snow, tilting it northwards so that he would know the direction when he got on his feet again. Then he sank down into a snowdrift in the lee of a hill, with Leó by his side, lay down for a while and let it snow him under, drift well over him, then he raised himself to his hands and knees, arched his back to form a roof and rocked this way and that to push the snow aside. This would be his and Leó's house, a kind of a house. Then they sat there in their snow hole. Outside, the world raged.

At first it was nice and warm there in that tiny cave under the snow. Benedikt even allowed himself to nod off a little now and then. But when his frozen clothes thawed and the warmth faded from his body as he sat there in his wet rags, any comfort he'd felt was gone. But he had to rest; that's why he sat there. And Benedikt rested as well as he could, dozed, but at the same time made sure not to drop off completely. Because once you fall asleep under the snow, hungry and exhausted, there is a great likelihood you will not wake up again to this life.

Suddenly he woke from his slumber. And knew at once that he could no longer sit there like that. So he and Leó started working their way back out of the drift, knocking down the snow around them and toiling their way up and out, four to six feet. And where was his staff now? It was nowhere to be found; the snow had swallowed it. It was tempting to crawl back down into the cave, to stay in the drift. Because the wind was even worse than before, and he estimated the temperature to be minus thirty, instead of the usual minus twenty. But now it was do or die. If he gave up now, it would not be for today, but for all days. Then, once the drifts melted, he would be found there – if he was found at all. No, the escape from the weather and whatever warmth he might have down there would be too dearly bought. Here, there was only one possible hope of salvation: to find his hole – his pot, his burrow. If he didn't find it, it would go for him as it did for so many sheep up here through the ages – no one found them, until the following year or the year after, their bleached bones were discovered blown clean of the sludge of life somewhere in the desolate sand.

Seeking out Eitill and the other sheep was out of the question today. Today's task was more limited than that. Now, it was about saving his own life. The frost bit into Benedikt's flesh through his wet clothes and the storm was on the verge of suffocating him, exasperated by the fact that his beard was frozen around his mouth. He took out his knife and sawed it off, otherwise he would never work loose the ice capsule that was about to close off his mouth and breathing. How they found his hole in the earth would be difficult to explain. Benedikt didn't know – and besides, it was Leó who found it. Suddenly Leó stopped walking and started scraping at the snow, and sure enough, Benedikt got down on all fours and groped around, groped the hatch free. And they descended and were saved. Benedikt went to light his tallow candle and stove immediately, but the matches were wet, didn't ignite. Benedikt laid them against his bare body, sat and dozed a little as they dried, gnawed a little frozen meat and bread and butter, but his mouth was too dry, he could hardly get it down. So he sat again and dozed. Then the matches were dry. And now he got the candle lit and the stove on the boil. What coffee is, know only those who have drunk it in a hole under the ground at minus thirty degrees in the middle of a desert of storms and mountains. And now he could even dry his clothes.

As he ate and drank, he inventoried his provisions. He still had four pieces of meat left, and quite a bit of butter. He also had a little sugar, but at that moment, he was drinking the last of his coffee. That's the way it was. And tomorrow was Monday, and the day after tomorrow Christmas Eve.

Is there more to tell of Benedikt and his twenty-seventh Advent trek? There must be. We can hardly leave him there in the hole, as abandoned by God and men as he already is, to all appearances.

It should be said that the next day, that is, on the Monday, hope woke in him that so much snow had piled up in the Jökulsá River that he could cross it on his skis and reach Jökull – it being 23 December, the Feast of St Þorlákur. But despite the frost and snowfall, the Jökulsá River turned out to be free of both ice and snow.

Furthermore, it ought to be said that when he then decided to set off straight for the settlement, to see if he could make it home before Christmas Eve, he came across a few more sheep, which it was impossible for him simply to leave, at least not until they'd been brought under Eitill's protection. And when this was taken care of, his strength for that day was at an end, making him glad to get back to his hole in the ground.

We would do well to report, too, that the day of Christmas Eve was spent moving Eitill and his group a touch closer to the settlement; that Benedikt and Leó celebrated Christmas Eve with each other in the hole, that on Christmas Day the weather was calm, but with a dense snowfall that delayed Benedikt and the sheep even more, that the wind started blowing harder towards evening and that another night was spent in the hole, and that the day after Christmas passed like Christmas Day itself. But that evening, on the last stretch of his journey, Benedikt gave up – old, tired and useless, he said of himself – gave up, left the sheep in Eitill's care and headed for the settlement – old, tired and useless.

Late in the evening he reached Botn. And was received as if he'd risen from the dead. But he didn't reply to the many words of welcome – where was young Benedikt? But young Benedikt wasn't at home. He'd gone to visit folk on neighbouring farms, without specifying his errand.

Oh – I was going to ask him to go back up with me soon, when the moon comes out again, said Benedikt.

No, young Benedikt wasn't at home. But the next morning it was reported at Botn that he'd taken a couple of young men with him and gone to the mountains. And before evening, he'd returned with the flock of sheep – and they had made shoes for Eitill, tied leather shoes around his hooves, which had been cut and bloodied by constantly being the first to trudge through the drifts and break their sharp crusts of snow. It was a sight worth seeing when they met in the homefield at Botn, old Benedikt and his Eitill. And young Benedikt, too.

Thank you, namesake, said old Benedikt,

who wasn't really the type of man for adding much more.

That day, a number of farmers from the area who'd grown anxious about Benedikt and hadn't heard of his return had agreed to meet at Botn and head to the mountains to search for him, and indeed for the younger men, too.

Facing that group stood young Benedikt, with a steady gaze and his head held high. Let our thanks go to whom it belongs, he replied to his older namesake.

And so, this Advent journey was concluded, the service to the community was brought to an end, and Benedikt was back among other people – for a time.

Afterword

It appears as if it does not take much in terms of contents to create a masterpiece, a book that is timeless. A man roams the woods with a gun and a dog, mutters a few things about nature, falls in love with a woman, and ends up shooting himself; a middle-aged writer takes a short break from writing, goes to Venice, falls in love with a teenage boy, loses his grip on life, and dies; a man wanders the wilderness with a dog and a wether in December, searching for sheep, gets caught in a storm but makes it back to civilisation alive.

Here I have described the contents of three books – novellas. This may not look like much, but a book's contents are seldom the most important thing about them; more important, perhaps, is their execution – a simple truth that tends to be forgotten. The three books to which I refer are *Pan* by Knut Hamsun, *Death in Venice* by Thomas Mann and *Advent* by Gunnar Gunnarsson.[*] Little further will be said here about Hamsun's and Mann's books – I shall resist the temptation, because at the moment it is Gunnar who matters. Gunnar, Benedikt, Leó and Eitill; it is so good to walk in moonlight amidst mountains. Yet first I must take a short detour before I head into the wilderness, on the heels of this trinity.

There's nothing like a first impression

I may have heard of Gunnar Gunnarsson first when I was in secondary school in Keflavík, but I don't clearly remember having done so, mainly because I've forgotten most things from those years: the knots that I learned in my seamanship course, algebra, etc. I first came into contact with Gunnar's writing when given the chore of wiping things clean at home. Gunnar's collected works, published in the sixties, stood lined up on one shelf,

---

[*] *Advent* (originally published in Danish in 1936) was previously published in English as *The Good Shepherd* (Bobbs-Merrill, 1940).

and I made sure not to touch the books with the moist cloth: eight thick volumes with rather small print. That's how I, thirteen years old, met him, in a single-family home in Keflavik. Every week for several years afterwards, I stood over his oeuvre, with the exception of his short stories, whenever I wiped off that shelf – yet I never opened a book by Gunnar until we were assigned to read him at university ten years later. It never occurred to me, at least not in any real earnestness, to read anything by Gunnar after I became hooked on literature; we all have our shortcomings, indeed – yet perhaps there are also other explanations.

In the literature of every nation there are certain works, let's call them pinnacles, monoliths, that are so dear to readers that their greatness, and presence, are nearly taken for granted – seemingly escaping any need for critique or even discussion. Gunnar's most renowned books, *The Church on the Mountain* (*Kirken paa bjerget*, 1923–28), *Guillemot* (*Svartfugl*, 1929) and *Advent*, are such works – pinnacles – yet while not being so, at the same time.* We who live here upon the outermost sea have perhaps never

* *Guillemot* was previously published in English as *The Black Cliffs* (University of Wisconsin, 1967).

truly come to terms with the Nobel Prize that Halldór Laxness was awarded in 1955; since then, there has been an imbalance in our perceptions and discussions of literature. A Nobel Prize can be dangerously big for a small country – our one and only mountain, we say of Halldór Laxness, as if there were just one mountain in all of Iceland – perhaps Herðubreið. Not Esja, not Kaldbakur, nor any of the 'fells': Sauðafell, Reykjafell. Yet those who care know that the very best in Gunnar Gunnarsson, as well as Þórbergur Þórðarson (1889–1974), of course, stands in every respect on a par with the pinnacles in Halldór Laxness' oeuvre; a simple truth that the Nobel Prize removed from the equation. It's another matter entirely that Halldór displays more faces than these writers, and that his career was more wide-reaching.

No, I never read Gunnar until my early twenties, when I began studying at the University of Iceland. I did, of course, read contemporary authors enthusiastically, yet when I looked over the history of Icelandic literature I beheld just the one mountain, apart, perhaps, from the peculiar Þórbergur Þórðarson. If my thoughts ever wandered to Gunnar, it would have been in the form of his collected works, the eight thick volumes. For me, he existed in an off-putting collection, not in particular books. I know of several others in the dedicated literati of my generation who hesitated, and still hesitate, in the face of weighty series, uncertain of where to begin, reluctant to be confronted with thousands of pages. Yet there is another factor that complicates matters considerably: Gunnar Gunnarsson wrote most of his works in Danish, not Icelandic. At the age of eighteen, he went to Denmark to study – a farmer's son from Iceland who had in fact published two thin volumes of poetry. He was a writer, and did not want to be anything other than a writer; for him, to live was to write – and vice versa. At the time, however, Iceland was a poor and relatively underdeveloped country; it was part of the Danish kingdom, with Copenhagen as its capital, and it was there that Icelanders had, for centuries, attended university. Gunnar could of course read Danish by the time he went abroad, yet he spoke it little and wrote it even less. He did, however, have a burning ambition: he wanted to make his living by writing, but since that was impossible in Iceland, he left, and managed in the space of just several years to gain a perfect grasp on Danish – so perfect that in the 1920s, he was among the most well-known and popular writers in the Danish language. Gunnar's Icelandic readers are, therefore, now faced with three options: to read his works in Danish, which few people do today; to read them in others' translations – for example, those of Halldór Laxness; or to read them in Gunnar's own translations. In his advanced years, Gunnar began to translate all of his own books; to transform, as an elderly man, what he had written as a youth. Thus, we are now confronted with three editions of his books, which of course also helps to complicate things, or even to hinder access to these books. Most people choose to read the translations, although Gunnar's written Danish is beautiful; yet then there is still the question of which translation to use: his own or another's.

Author of two worlds

Gunnar developed as a writer in an environment radically different to what most Icelandic authors knew. The century's conflicts, the existential angst in the wake of the First World War and world affairs in the 1920s hit closer to home for Gunnar than his contemporaries in Iceland, who perhaps concerned themselves more with tussock-levelling tractors and Danish rule than world affairs. Whether it was because of his place of residence or his disposition – these two, perhaps, being inseparable – Gunnar seemed to have put more thought into the narrative form itself than his colleagues did here in Iceland; he was more focused, his books better structured, more conscientious. He was, simultaneously, an author of two worlds: an Icelander who wrote in Danish, living in a big city, yet always with the Icelandic countryside as the setting of his books. The city where he lived, Copenhagen, rarely appears in his works, yet when it does, it is quite bulky – as, for instance, in *The Inexperienced Travelers* (*Den uerfarne rejsende*, 1927), the final volume of *The Church on the Mountain*. This work's first two volumes, *Ships in the Sky* (*Skibe på himlen*, 1925) and *The Night and the Dream* (*Natten og drømmen*, 1926) have received praise, while *The Inexperienced Travelers* is considered inferior. This judgement is possibly infected by people's belief that writers, in their autobiographies, put their best energies into describing their childhood years – while what comes afterwards lacks a certain gusto. This has been said about Gunnar, as it has also been said of the final volume in Maxim Gorky's magnificent books about his childhood and youthful years, books that undoubtedly influenced Gunnar's writing of *The Church on the Mountain*. These great works by different authors have elements in common, and they both glow with the dark and bright fires lit by the sparks created when reality and fiction are hurled together. I've always had the feeling that *The Inexperienced Travelers* was not given its due; it's our *Hunger*, and if viewed in a broader European context, it could be seen to stand somewhere between Hamsun's work (on the deprivation and starvation brought about by poverty) and Rilke's 'upper-class starvation': the story of Malte Laurids Briggen.

Despite the fact that Gunnar never does, in a certain sense, leave home as a novelist, always choosing a thoroughly Icelandic setting, the fate of the wider world, the confused Europe in the first part of the twentieth century, seems always to exert a pervasive influence on his works. Yet I've sometimes wondered whether Gunnar's emphasis on Icelandic material – the weather, the wilderness – became more pronounced due to his place of residence; whether Iceland itself, its people and environment, became, in a sense, 'greener' or 'fonder' – more vivid – in response to distance, as well as, perhaps, because his readers, Danes and then Germans, were enamoured by and sought after descriptions of such material. Do these two things, the influence of distance and the thirst of readers for descriptions of the North, explain Gunnar's incredibly long description of the *vikivaki* ring-dance early in his novel *Vikivaki* (1932)? The chapter containing the description is a peculiar bastard. Few Icelandic books begin as originally as *Vikivaki*, yet we can say without hesitation that the novel loses almost all of its unique, peculiar atmosphere after dozens of pages of rustic romance. Why? I can't shake the feeling that with *Vikivaki*, the influence of distance – the strong, even sentimental pull of home – numbed Gunnar's sense of self-critique, to his misfortune. This, in fact, means that I cannot possibly agree with those who consider *Vikivaki* among his best books. The idea behind the novel is certainly brilliant, if not fantastic, yet the same does not apply to its composition, leaving the book considerably inferior to the three jewels: *The Church on the Mountain, Guillemot* and *Advent*.

A man goes to the mountains and is then printed in 250,000 copies

I don't know how many times I've read *Advent*, but for a span of about fifteen years, I read the story of Benedikt and his companions every Christmas, starting on the Feast of St Þorlákur (December 23) and finishing on Christmas Day, reading slowly, enjoying the experience as much as one might enjoy sitting and chatting with old friends. Various things have been said about *Advent* since it was published, first in German in 1936, then in Danish, and finally in Icelandic translation in 1939. No book of Gunnar's has travelled as widely, to more countries than you can count on both hands. It was, for instance, printed in 250,000 copies in the United States, and there is certainly something to the idea that *Advent* was the spark for *The Old Man and the Sea* by Ernest Hemingway.

The genesis of *Advent* has its own special history.

On 10 December, 1925, a group of men headed to the mountains in the Eastfjords of Iceland to search for sheep. One of the men was named Benedikt Sigurjónsson, nicknamed Mountain-Bensi, a man with the wilderness in his blood. Six years later, an account of Mountain-Bensi's hazardous journey in the wilderness, written by Þórður Jónsson, appeared in the magazine *Eimreið*. In this account, Bensi continues the search for livestock — first horses, then sheep – on his own in the Mývatn Wilderness after his companions head back to human haunts with a flock of sheep on 13 December. After enduring great hardships, Mountain-Bensi returns to the farms on the Second Day of Christmas (26 December) to find that folk have begun making preparations to search for him. Gunnar apparently read the story in Denmark, and when the magazine *Julesne* asked him to write a story set in Iceland, he wrote the short story 'The Good Shepherd', based on Þórður's account of Mountain-Bensi. The short story is 'mainly a poetically stylised retelling of the account of Mountain-Bensi's journey', wrote the critic Ólafur Jónsson. Five years passed, and then the German publishing house Reclam contacted Gunnar and asked him to write a novella for their series Reclam Universal Bibliothek – and *Advent* was born. The story itself, its protagonist, Benedikt, and his search for sheep in the wilderness in the second-most vicious month of the Icelandic winter, thus has its roots in what we call reality, as opposed to fiction, although the distinction between them is more dubious than many believe, so dubious that trying to draw clear lines between the two could directly jeopardise one's mental health. It is of course nice to know the stories behind books, the models for their characters, the events that set fictional accounts in motion, creating worlds parallel to this one; such information is enjoyable, yet is irrelevant, all the same – chaff – because what matters is the world of the book, the literary creation, and books should always be read on their terms, as they stand or fall in and of themselves, not elsewise. Yet for those who wish to acquaint themselves with Gunnar's working methods, reflect on the genesis of books and in doing so attempt to better understand the writer behind the words, it doesn't hurt to compare 'The Good Shepherd' and *Advent*, for by doing so, we get an unexpected chance to snoop around in Gunnar's studio, observe him whittling ideas, giving them greater depth, see how he gradually distances himself from events and characters that set everything in motion, distances himself from models and creates his own world. We see how he whittles down a long account in 'The Good Shepherd' – half a biography, almost – to three lines in *Advent*; here I mean the description of the relationship between Benedikt and Sigríður of Botn. A dramatic story, turbulent emotions, an account of a shipwreck and an unusual reconciliation – all of this is written in such a way that it seems almost to hover invisibly in the words; so masterful is Gunnar with the style of *Advent*, at ease and disciplined at once, that he manages to squeeze it all in without us noticing, simply by creating an atmosphere that we sense, that we breathe in – that we live.

A man roams the wilderness with a dog and a wether in December, searching for sheep, gets caught in a storm yet makes it back to human habitations alive; this is the story of *Advent*. Simple on the surface. I wouldn't exactly call what's below the surface complex, yet the book certainly does have depth and fertility. The story itself, in all of its simplicity, is excellent and classic: man facing the elements. To that theme, however, are added the style and the author's reflections, partly motivated by the story, partly not, at once familiar and deeply philosophical, opening up to the reader through simple acts:

> And as they went in, he pinched the candle's wick between two fingers. It's most merciful to a candle not to allow it to languish uselessly.

From Blicher to Conrad

Stylistically, *Advent* is something of an adventure tale. Gunnar was a master stylist, as witnessed in his books. At times garrulous, even to an extreme, as in *The Church on the Mountain*; hard and coarse as in *Sonata of the Sea* (*Sonate ved havet*, 1955); yet nowhere as straightforward and downright beautiful as in *Advent*. No man, however, is an island in literature; the same sort of style appears in different authors. I don't know how far back it's possible to trace it – perhaps to the Dane Steen Steensen Blicher, who wrote in the first part of the nineteenth century, and whom

Gunnar greatly admired, among other things translating one of his novels, *Præsten I Vejlbye* (*The Rector of Veilbye*, originally published in 1829). It's a unique style; I don't know whether it can be called Nordic, but it achieves a certain perfection in Knut Hamsun, the matchless wizard who influenced so many different writers. Hemingway dreamed of writing like Hamsun, and his admiration for the Norwegian's style could lend a bit of support to the idea that *Advent* appealed to him so strongly that *The Old Man and the Sea* was born. Other authors, however, might be mentioned: Gunnar, of course; Halldór Laxness; the Faeroese William Heinesen; and the Dane Martin A. Hansen. But where does this style come from; why were Nordic authors drawn to it? Is it the combination of weather and light, long, dark winters, and summer nights so bright that they give nothing rest? A dreamy realism, poetic narrative, quiet in nature, yet nevertheless accommodating the scream that Edvard Munch captured on canvas; composure that is a kind of complacency, likely sprung from depression. In this style, darkness does not reign, but neither does light; perhaps it is twilight.

One element that marks *Advent* so strongly, as well as *The Church on the Mountain*, I might add, is Gunnar's description of the weather. I can hardly recall having read – how shall I say it – such strong, convincing descriptions of storms as Gunnar's – except perhaps those of Joseph Conrad. I'm often reminded of Gunnar when reading Conrad and encountering his descriptions of the fury of storms on the open sea, and likewise, I'm reminded of Conrad when Gunnar starts describing storms in the mountains. Both writers strike such familiar chords in the reader with these descriptions of the raging forces of nature that he cowers instinctively, which is perhaps a natural reaction when confronted with forces over which we have no control; something in the deepest recesses of our memories commands us to cower, make ourselves smaller, revert to tiny mammals huddling in our holes at the approach of something incredibly big: a dinosaur or meteorite. Is there not an affinity between Gunnar and Conrad? And I don't just mean in their unique ability to describe the weather. Gunnar was an Icelander who wrote in Danish, a language that he learned following adolescence; Conrad was a Pole who wrote in English, a language that he also learned following adolescence. Both are known for their grasp of language, surpassing most native authors in that regard; both are philosophical and put a great deal into structuring their narratives – novelists par excellence. Gunnar was undoubtedly familiar with Conrad, most of the Pole's books having been published in Danish translation by the time Gunnar set foot in Denmark, presumably to conquer the world.

On deep-rooted familiarity

Benedikt travels with a dog and a wether; they are his companions. An account of a man who travels alone, page after page, and what's more, without his head full of ancient wisdom, like Aschenbach in *Death in Venice* – wisdom that proves, of course, inadequate against the violence of emotions. This man, Benedikt, who knows little about Greek gods, even less about German philosophers, is certainly caught up in the violence of emotions, like Aschenbach, yet proves victorious – and an author who creates such a character needs to solve various technical problems. For how, if the author does not wish to intrude constantly, is he to fill the pages with words and actions? By what means can he create life and movement around Benedikt, who tramps his way, first up from the farmland, then alone through the wilderness, which can be so antagonistic to all of mankind? Alone? What am I saying? He is so far from being alone – there are three of them, the Holy Trinity! Yet it is one thing to have a dog and wether in one's company, another thing to give them such clear, personal characteristics as Leó and Eitill have. You generally forget that what you have are a man and two animals – in your mind they are three companions – not a man and animals. Eitill is serious, grave, yet trusty and gritty, while Leó is something of a clown, albeit indispensable when the going gets tough. He is in fact the book's scene-stealer; Gunnar inserts half a sentence in connection with him here and there, simple observations about dogs, yet in a way that makes the reader smile and feel for a moment as if the world is darned amusing. Gunnar actually removes all doubt at the start of the story that the three are first and foremost companions, not a man and two animals, and does it in such a way that the reader fully understands that between the three lies the kind of thread that makes life valuable, the world a place worth inhabiting:

> For a number of years, these three had been inseparable when it came to such treks and had gradually got to know each other, inside and out, with the in-depth familiarity that is perhaps only obtainable between completely unrelated species of animals, such that no shadow of one's own self, one's own blood, own wishes or desires confuses or obscures things.

This description of the relationship between Benedikt, Leó and Eitill is also an excellent example of how Gunnar expands the world of the book; simple things are given familiar – I would almost say universal – appeal. We do not simply have a narrative of incidents and events, but also reflections on life itself, on the innermost nature of things. Here is another example: Benedikt has come to Botn on his first day, with the entire trip before him. Botn is situated highest of all farms in the area, with farmland below, and the wilderness itself above. Benedikt is thus at a kind of border, and the following short passage contains not only poetic philosophy, but also a subtle and dramatic description of the essential difference between being down among people and up in the wilderness. Here, the reader can sense what awaits Benedikt:

> People who walk together in darkness disappear from each other in such a peculiar way. Yet that isolation in darkness is different from the isolation you feel in the mountains. Down here among the farms it isn't so absolute; you can hear voices other than your own, feel nearby breaths. The profound desolation of outer space and the stony depths doesn't chill you to the roots of your hair.

Fertility of the reader's mind

Advent has been interpreted in various ways. A review in 1938 stated, 'This is a magnificent winter ode,' which 'holds one's attention, despite the thinness of the story itself'. The poet Matthías Johannessen says that a recurring theme in the works of Gunnar is the place of man in existence, to 'be responsible, seek the truth and essence of existence, try to understand man's place – Gunnar

Gunnarsson has wrestled with these questions in all of his works.' I must confess that I have occasionally felt that this wrestling match made Gunnar's fiction unnecessarily cumbersome, even hindered him as a creative writer, preventing him from seeking new methods in form, as if he forgot that the search for fiction and the search for truth are one and the same – if not the same arm, then the same body. Or, as someone has written: 'It isn't healthy for an author to think too much; let's leave that to the philosophers.' This, of course, doesn't apply to Gunnar's best works, *Guillemot* being an excellent example – a dark and serious book in which the weighty search for truth sweeps a person along with it, like a dark river.

There is much to the works of Gunnar; they are deep and spring to mind at the unlikeliest of occasions: quotations and characters, even entire books. I recently spoke with a writer who said that he frequently found himself thinking about *Blessed are the Simple* (*Salige er de enfoldige*), which was published in 1920, whenever avian or swine flu came up in conversation, as if that memorable book were a direct description of the pandemic possibly threatening the human race. Gunnar is ambiguous, and *Advent* has likewise been interpreted in various ways. Some have claimed that Gunnar purposefully wove the life and message of Christ into the story – that Benedikt's journey ought to be seen as an allegory of the life and message of Christ. There's no new evidence that Gunnar Gunnarsson ever thought to any great degree about Christ and the Bible; yet *Blessed are the Simple* does take place, for instance, over seven days, which is of course a reference to the biblical account of creation, and certainly one thinks of Christ and his messages while reading *Advent*. Benedikt is a humble commoner, but it's one thing to be humble, and entirely another to be simple. Some would say that Benedikt has a strong natural and emotional intelligence – he is extremely sensitive to nature and his animals, knows the blades of grass in the summer heaths as well as the winter storms up in the wilderness; he is a person who understands innately the core of the message of Christ. Benedikt has the rare capacity to ignore the chaff – he is in fact unaware of it; the core of the message is simply obvious to him. On the other hand, warning bells sound in my mind when Benedikt is described as an imitation of Christ, and *Advent* as a saint's life. I understand very

107

well that some people find it tempting to interpret the novella in this way – Gunnar frequently makes reference, directly or indirectly, to the Bible, which is intimately familiar to Benedikt, being part of his family readings, particularly at this time of year, Advent itself; yet it is highly questionable to make these references a principal issue – the main point of the story. A book that gains a reputation for being a modern saint's life, an allegory of the life of Christ, is at risk of going stale in the minds of readers; it is prevented from being interpreted in other ways, and even worse, the book will no longer be read on its own terms, the terms of literary fiction. The reader dresses themself in their Sunday best and reads with the humility of a communicant, but this is how one must never approach literature, whose continued existence depends on the fertility of the reader's mind.

Jón Kalman Stefánsson
Translated by Philip Roughton